5/97

NOW I WILL NEVER LEAVE THE DINNER TABLE

by Jane Read Martin and Patricia Marx

illustrated by Roz Chast

HarperCollins*Publishers*

Library of Congress Cataloging-in-Publication Data

Martin, Jane Read.

Now I will never leave the dinner table / by Jane Read Martin and Patricia Marx ;
illustrated by Roz Chast.

p.   cm.

Sequel to: Now everybody really hates me.

Summary: When her perfect older sister forces her to remain at the dinner table
until she finishes her spinach, a young girl broods about being stuck there forever
and devises a plan to get rid of her sister.

ISBN 0-06-024794-0. — ISBN 0-06-024795-9 (lib. bdg.)

[1. Sisters—Fiction.   2. Spinach—Fiction.   3. Food habits—Fiction.]   I. Marx,
Patricia (Patricia A.)   II. Chast, Roz, ill.   III. Title.

PZ7.M363166Np   1996   94-3209

[E]—dc20   CIP

                                                                          AC

Typography by Christine Kettner

2   3   4   5   6   7   8   9   10

❖

To our sisters, Ann and Sarah Jane
—J.R.M. and P.M.

To Ian and Nina
—R.C.

I am at the dinner table and I am never leaving.

Here is what my sister Joy, the bossy baby-sitter, says: The
reason I am still at the dinner table is that I put all my spinach
in my pocket. Now I must stay until I take a bite of spinach.
And swallow it.

Here is what I say:

#1) I did not put *all* my spinach in my pocket. I gave some to Sarge.

#2) In my opinion, spinach should be put back in the ground where it came from.

#3) I will never finish my spinach. Even if that means sitting here until I am grown up with children of my own.

Just a few minutes ago I made up my mind: I, Patty Jane
Pepper, will stay at the table for the *rest* of my *life*. . . .

I have done it before.

Let me tell you about my big sister Joy.

Joy is smart. Joy is beautiful. Joy has perfect hair.

Everybody loves Joy. Except for me. I call Joy . . .

Joy never has what I call fun. Joy does not like to do spider
art. Joy does not like to get dizzy with our little brother,
Theodore, and me. Joy does not even like mud.

Joy, of course, loves spinach. She loves spinach so much
that she invented seventeen ways to cook it.

Joy also discovered a new chemical for her science project.
For my science project, I tried to invent an Anti-Sister Ray Gun.

Joy also won the Table Manners Medal. Joy eats candy with a fork. And a knife.

Joy always puts a napkin in her lap, even when she's sleeping.

Joy's hobby is folding her shirts.

And tattling on me, of course.

I have been thinking it over and I have decided that Joy would be happier living with the Hills down the street. They have so much in common.

Let me tell you about Mr. and Mrs. Hill. I am not sure of their exact ages, but I would say approximately 123 years old (each). They have no children *whatsoever*.

I will help Joy pack if I ever leave the table.

Tomorrow, our house will be Joy-free. Yea!

I will use Joy's room solely for my gum chain collection.

And what will I do with Joy's diary? Rent it out for $2.00 a day.

At dinner, I will eat her dessert. But I will not eat her spinach.

Soon my parents will be home and I will tell them how Joy imprisoned me at the table with only bread and water to eat (not counting dinner). Then Joy will be really sorry.

Oh, life without Joy will be so sweet! If I ever leave the table.

Then again, without Joy . . .

Whom will I seesaw with if Sondra, Theodore, Nina, Edie, Sarah Jane, Ann, Lynne, Kathy, Janice, Becky, Maryann, Rebecca, Diane, Marion, Marlaine, Victoria, Jeri, Laura, Carol, Robin and Catherine, Meg, Christy, Alexandra, Jessica, Julie, Jennifer, Lorraine, Ginny, Elaine, P.Q., Mary, Lillian, Kim, Ricki, Jean, Suzi, Liz, Frances, Rosie, Sophie and Sophia, Joan, Julia, Emily, Lorrie, Taylor, Paige, Brooke, Amy, Sarah, Cora, Eliza, Kate, Lucy, Joanne, Susan, Deborah, Rachel Lewis, *and* Sarge are all sick?

But let's face it. I will never see another seesaw
for the rest of my life. I will be stuck at the table forever
and ever and ever and ever until infinity.

At which point I will turn into a statue.

Then I will have to go live in a museum. Which means Joy
will have to pay to see me. Ha ha!

I wonder where my parents are. For they were supposed to be home from the Allens' at 8:00 and now it is precisely 8:03 and 34 seconds. Perhaps Mr. and Mrs. Allen will not let my parents leave until they finish *their* spinach.

You know, I was thinking. Spinach could be tasty if you stirred in some smooshed potato chips, a dash of grape juice, and plenty of ketchup.

Mmmm . . . I think I've stumbled upon an eighteenth way to cook spinach. A flair for discovering spinach recipes must run in our family. Wait until I show Joy.

Speaking of Joy, the Hills are awfully old to have a child, even one like Joy who is already a miniature old lady.

Perhaps it would be best for everyone if I allow Joy to remain here.

Yes, Joy may stay . . .

Unless the next time she baby-sits she tries to make me eat succotash.